Rogue Reynard

Rogue Reynard

Being a tale of the Fortunes and
Misfortunes and divers Misdeeds
of that great Villain, Baron
Reynard, the Fox, and
how he was served
with King Lion's
Justice.

Based upon The Beast Saga

Written by Andre Norton
and Pictured by Laura Bannon

Reynard the Fox

Houghton Mifflin Company · Boston
The Riverside Press · Cambridge
1947

To
My Mother and Father
and to
Phyllis
who fostered my acquaintance with
Rogue Reynard

Contents

Contents

Chapter the first

WHICH TELLETH HOW KING LION KEPT COURT AND BARON REYNARD APPEARED NOT THEREAT

In those days, when King Lion ruled the Great Forest and gave justice to all who asked it of him, it was his custom to hold once a year — at the falling of the leaves — a court at which all Forest animals appeared. Then were all disputes among them settled, the boundaries of hunting lands for the next year set, and all other matters of note discussed. And when the summons to gather for this court went forth — carried by the rabbits of the wood-land who were the King's own Heralds — no animal, unless gravely ill, refused to answer it. That is, no ani-mal had, until the year when Baron Reynard, the Fox, tested the King's power.

Baron Reynard had no desire to appear at court be-cause there would be many there who could rise to speak against him for his deeds during the past year. And among those who might complain in full, loud voices was that powerful lord Count Lupus, the Wolf. For evil had been the trick Reynard had played upon one of the Count's own household.

So when the Rabbit cried aloud the royal summons before the door of Baron Reynard's manor-house, the Fox said to his good wife:

'This time we shall not go to court, but shall bide snug within our own four walls.'

Now at this speech Lady Fox was alarmed, for she feared the might of the King.

'And if you do not go, then will King Lion send for you to be brought unto him, and that will be a fearsome thing——'

But the Baron smiled at her fears. 'Leave it to me, lady wife. For what was I given sharp wits, if not to think my way out of such dangers? Also, have we not good friends at court who will warn us of trouble before it appears? And not the least of these is Squire Weasel, who has no reason to like the King's justice any better than I do.'

Thus, when all the animals gathered, from the boundaries and secret places of the Great Forest to its heart where King Lion sat enthroned, the Fox, his lady wife, and their two cubs were not among them, but lay snugly at home within their manor-house and waited what would come. But Lady Fox was still sore afraid, although she had learned not to speak of her fear to the Baron.

When all the Forest dwellers were assembled, the King ordered them to be numbered by his Earl Marshal. And Bruin, the Bear, did so speedily, saying to King Lion:

'All are here to do you honor, my liege lord, as is the custom, save Baron Reynard and those of his household. But their manor-house is afar and they may yet arrive.'

The Lion nodded. 'It is well. But if they come not by nooning, or send no message, then shall you deal with them according to the law. Now let the court be declared open.'

And that was done so that every animal might speak

out concerning what lay upon his heart. And to their complaints the Lion listened well and dealt justice thereafter so that all were satisfied with his dealing.

While he was so doing, Earl Marshal Bruin went privately to the Hare, who was master of the King's Heralds and asked concerning Baron Reynard, and if the court summons had been properly called at the door of his manor-house. Then the Hare in turn summoned the Rabbit who had been the messenger in that part of the wood and questioned him. It was so learned that the messenger had called the summons loudly and true before Reynard's gate even as the King's law bade. Likewise did the Bear learn that Reynard had made no excuse for not appearing at court. And he made note of both these matters to tell the King.

When the hour of nooning came, the animals were urged to a banquet spread before the King's judgment seat. And there they ate according to their tastes while the King rested and spoke with those of his great lords who were gathered about his person. And then did the Earl Marshal say:

'My lord, Baron Reynard and his household have not yet arrived, nor has he sent any excuse for his absence. I have examined your Herald and the court summons was cried loud and truly at his door, even as your laws provide. What is your will that we do in this matter?'

The Lion looked about the circle of his lords and asked:

'What reason could keep the Fox from this court?'

And Count Lupus, the Wolf, answered right grimly: 'Reason enough, my lord. There are full many assembled here this day who have come to cry for justice against this black rascal, and among them I stand.'

Then indeed was the Lion astonished and his wrath began to rise.

'If I find it true that the Fox comes not to court to escape the naming of his deeds, then will he be hunted down by the might of my law! Never have we spoken against one of us who is not here to answer. But today, when the feasting is over, let Baron Reynard's name be called aloud so that any who have aught against him may say so. That is by our will, Earl Marshal.'

The Bear bowed and went away to arrange it so.

Chapter the second

WHICH TELLETH HOW COUNT LUPUS ACCUSED THE FOX OF A SORRY MISDEED

Thus, when the feasting was done and all the court was assembled once more in solemn order, the Earl Marshal arose and held his sword high, in this way signifying that grave justice was to be done. And the Hare, as Chief Herald, called out the name of Baron Reynard so that any who had wrongs from him might testify before the King.

Quick was Count Lupus to arise and signal for King Lion's attention. And it was granted him that he might tell his tale.

'I cry upon our Lord King for justice in the name of one of my household,' he began, 'namely, my lady wife who has been most grievously misused by this villain Fox — so injured that she needs must keep her room and go no longer into company among those of her rank.

'It happened thus: Last year in the months of freezing when the waters of river and pond were solid ice, Baron Reynard chanced to pass our castle and behind him walked one of his varlets laden down with a great catch of fine fresh fish. Now my lady wife has a taste for fish and when she looked upon these she was much excited, so she straightway called out to Baron Reynard: "Ha, neighbor Reynard, how came you by that wondrous catch of fine fresh fish? Pond and river are ice and we have had no fish on our table these four months or more."

'This rogue then smiled and spoke her fair in return, saying: "Indeed do I feel for you, Lady Wolf, not to have such dainty, tender flesh for your eating. Were it not that my own lady wife is ailing and has been urged by the apothecary to eat naught but fish, I would gladly leave you three or four of these. But at least I can put you in the way of getting some for yourself."

'Then was my lady amazed and eager and she came down to that rascal, demanding that he give her the secret of his fishing. So he sent his varlet on with the fish and then he took my wife down to the river — she, poor witless loon, believing all that he said to her with his lying mouth.

'Once there he, with his own paws, chopped a hole in the ice of midstream. And then he said to my wife that if she wished fish, she needs must sit above the hole with her tail in the water. When she felt a fish bite upon her tail, she could then draw it out, and that would happen speedily. Then he added that he must get home to his poor wife, and, wishing Lady Wolf luck in her fishing, he departed.

'But having left her sight he went secretly to that village of Men which borders our Forest and there he cried out that a Wolf was caught in the ice on the river. As all in this court know, the hands of Men are ever against us. So they were joyful at such news, and, taking clubs, they went out upon the river to hunt down the wolf.

'Meanwhile, the ice, after the manner of ice, had frozen fast about my lady's tail, holding her tight prisoner, so that she was weeping sorely and lamenting her fate and her foolishness at listening to the tales of Rogue Reynard. Drawn by my poor wife's loud cries, the Men came upon her soon and then they fell to and beat her full hard so that she was like to die, until with all her strength she burst forth and got away—but only because she tore off her tail, which remained in the ice.

'Now, shorn of her beauty, she remains ever in her chamber and weeps so often that she is worn as thin as a sapling shadow and is like to die of her sorrow and shame—going no more out into company or allowing even the children of our own house to see her in her distress. And all of this because of the lies and trickery of Reynard, the Fox. So do I, confident in the King's justice, call for a settling of this upon the Fox's own body. Let him lose his tail—that tail of which he is so proud—and see how it fares with him thereafter!'

And as the Wolf spoke, many animals murmured in agreement, for Reynard had but very few to speak for him then, since many of his sly evil practices had given the Forest dwellers cause to think all manner of ill against him. But the Lion frowned, believing that it was for him, the Forest King, to lay a proper punishment upon the Fox, and not for Count Lupus to suggest one. So he made no direct answer to the Wolf's plea. Only at his signal the Hare came forward again and called upon any who wished to speak against Reynard to do so.

Chapter the third

WHICH TELLETH HOW SIR CHANTICLEER CAME WITH HIS DAUGHTER TO CRY FOR JUSTICE

And the Hare was answered right speedily by one who came on slow dragging feet followed by others who bore among them a small coffin. And this grim casket they brought to the very foot of the throne. Then the chief mourner raised his head and threw back his black hood, and all saw that he was Sir Chanticleer Cock, an old and worthy nobleman much beloved by Forest folk. This knight had never committed a fault against any there, but had walked uprightly all his days, so that no animal could claim any wrong of his house; and thus he had won the respect and good will of all.

With his own claws Sir Chanticleer lifted up the lid of the coffin so that King Lion and those of his lords who were nearest could see what lay therein. And so they looked upon the body of the youngest daughter of Sir Chanticleer, she of whom the old Cock was the most fond.

'Aye, my King and lords,' he said in a low voice, much broken, 'it is she, my Pippet. Here she lies because of the villainy of Baron Reynard. I have brought her here that her silent lips might cry out for justice. Because it was the Fox who slew her. I beg you, allow me to speak against him in her name——'

And the Lion, horrified by the piteous sight and much moved by Sir Chanticleer's sorrow, replied:

'Say out all the matters concerning this, for if what you say can be proven, then will our justice move speedily against such a scoundrel, for he has no place in the Forest world.'

And to that a whisper of assent arose from all the court.

Sir Chanticleer bowed his head. But when he spoke it was in a clear, loud voice so that all could hear his tale.

'As all here know full well, I and my household dwell in Cockcrow Manor in the second Forest clearing. There have we lived at peace with all for many years. But of late Baron Reynard has crossed my lands and looked often into my gardens. At first I thought no evil of him, but then my son came to me with a strange story of Baron Reynard urging him out to hunt with him in the Forest. Now, as this court knows, we have no interest in hunting, nor do we go into the darker part of the Forest, so I could not understand this invitation of the Fox.

'But I bade all those of my household to keep well within the gates and walls of the manor and not to heed any invitations given them by Baron Reynard. My son is obedient, but he is not wise in the ways of the great world. So, when the next day Baron Reynard called to him again from the gate and urged a hunt, my son answered him with the truth — that his father had bade him not go beyond the walls of his own manor. Baron Reynard smiled and said that always it is well to obey one's parents, and he went away.

'The next morning while I was overseeing the labor in my fields, the Fox came to me and said that my son had told him of my wishes. He complimented me upon the obedience of my son, but added that he was sorry that such evil tidings concerning himself had reached me that I needs must forbid all friendliness between us.

'So fair did he speak and with such sense and feeling that I began to believe that I had been full foolish in my orders against him. And when nooning came I asked him to my board, where he did come and eat peacefully with my household, speaking so kindly to my lady wife and the children that they were greatly pleased and soon had a great liking for him.

'Several times did he so come and break bread with us until we thought no more of any strangeness about him. And my sons and daughters called him "good uncle" and loved him well. Thus did he lay the plans of his villainy.

'And when we feared him no more, nor even noted much his comings and goings, he came into my lady wife's inner garden where my dear Pippet was gathering roses and there he seized upon her to drag her forth. But she cried out mightily, so that her brothers and the varlets of my household ran in upon them. Thus Baron Reynard did not accomplish all of his foul design and have Pippet to hang in his larder. But when we raised her up we found her dead.

'That is my story of this base Fox, my King and lords. And now I cry, Justice! Justice! Let Reynard be dealt by as he has dealt with me and mine!'

Having so spoken, the old Cock drew his cowl over his head and, looking neither to the right hand nor to the left, went out from among them, those of his household carrying the small coffin behind him, while all the court was aroused to righteous wrath by such a black tale.

Chapter the fourth

WHICH TELLETH HOW EARL MARSHAL
BEAR WAS SENT TO FETCH THE VILLAIN
FOX WHO WAS FOREWARNED

mongst those who were raising their voices against this rogue Fox stood Squire Weasel. Now he was of a different mind, having an old friendship for Baron Reynard and being like unto him in the blackness of his heart. So he took thought that he must warn Reynard of the King's anger, that the Fox might be prepared to defend himself. And straightway the Weasel slipped through the crowd unnoted, and hurried by a little-known way to Reynard's manor-house.

Back at court Bruin Bear, the Earl Marshal, received the King's orders to ride into Baron Reynard's domain, rout out the rascal, and bring him to face the Lion's justice. And Bruin was glad, for many a day had he hated the Fox and his evil deeds and had longed to put an end to them. So armed and well mounted, but alone, he rode off, the good wishes of all speeding him on his way.

But he took the wide highway which King Lion had caused to be cut through the Forest, and this was the longer way. So that, long before he came into the dell where stood Fox Manor, the Weasel had reached there and had told Reynard the ill news of what had happened at court.

Upon hearing it, Reynard's lady wife did wail long and loud and speak to her mate wrathfully of the fate he had brought upon them. And he listened to her patiently until she was fair worn to fainting with her fears. Then he answered briskly enough:

'Do not so lose your courage, my sweet. For look who the King is sending to wrest me hence The Earl Marshal is mighty in battle, and, were I facing him claw to claw, tooth to tooth, you would have good reason to cry out. But his wits are not so keen as his fangs, and this is a matter of wits. I have a plan which will work well, that I swear to you. But let me speak with him and say naught yourself. And you, my good Squire Weasel, well indeed have you served me this day and that I shall not forget in a month, nay, nor in a year. However, it is best that you go swiftly back to court, lest some evil-minded hanger-on there remark your absence and spread words which will injure us both.'

The Weasel, seeing the wisdom of that, made his farewells and was safely away before the Earl Marshal came to the manor gates, which he did a full hour before sunset.

To Bruin's great surprise Baron Reynard threw the gates wide, coming out to meet him with every sign of pleasure, his jaws agrin in a smile. And he stood with meek patience while the Bear sternly repeated the King's orders. When the Earl Marshal had done, Reynard bowed and said:

'Honored am I and my house that you have come in person to deliver this sore order, my lord, when so easily you might have sent divers of your meaner varlets to wreak your will. Unhappy am I that I have been so slandered before the King and that so many ills have been reported against me when I was absent and could not reply to such lies. Indeed will I go with you that I may prove myself innocent and so wipe the slime from the name of Reynard. But night is now drawing in and the way is long. May I suggest that we rest and return in the morning when our road will be again well lighted?'

Now the road had been long and the ride tiring, and Bruin thought that there was no harm in this suggestion. Also Baron Reynard did not seem so great a villain when one saw him and listened to his courteous speech. So he was easily enough persuaded to agree to the Fox's advice.

Then again did Reynard hang his head in humbleness and there was shame in his voice when he spoke:

'Alas, this is but the poorest of Forest manors, my lord, and we are rustic folk not accustomed to entertaining the great ones of the earth within our walls. I have not even proper food and drink to set before such a one as the King's Earl Marshal, one whose lips are still greasy with the fine dishes of the King's own table. Therefore I shall not try to appease your hunger here. But beyond that fringe of saplings, my lord, is a full fine share of what your family esteems the highest—fresh honey. And it is yours for the eating——'

Then indeed did Bruin's heart lift as he thought of this fine treat and he forgot the dusty miles behind him, being all eagerness to take into his mouth these sweets. He moved readily toward the saplings and was impatient when the Fox detained him to say:

'But, my lord, these dainties belong to a Man and he has set a trap to catch any who would rob his hives. You will surely be caught unless you put your paws through the middle part of the standing log which is fastened before the shelf whereon the hives are set ——'

'Thank you, thank you, Baron Reynard, for your courtesy,' replied the Bear. 'I surely will do even as you have advised.' And he shouldered his way through the screen of saplings.

Chapter the fifth

WHICH TELLETH OF THE EARL MARSHAL'S PLIGHT AND HIS RETURN TO THE COURT

Beyond the saplings it was as the Fox had said. A long row of hives were set up tidily on a bench with before them a log fastened in a cradle of ropes. The Bear needed the advice of Reynard, thrusting his paws through the wide opening in the log to grasp at the hives.

But when he touched the log it snapped heavily together, holding him tight prisoner in spite of all his struggles. When this had happened, Baron Reynard, who had been watching from behind the bushes, ran to the Man's house and cried aloud at his door:

'Ho, neighbor, out to your hives! For there you have caught a robber bear!'

The Man, hearing the voice, thought it was one of his neighbors, and straightway he caught up a heavy club, telling his wife to go also and rouse the other men of the hamlet so that they could deal hardly with the bear. She, doing as her husband bade, brought a goodly crowd of laborers, and they went into the honey clearing and there found Bruin moaning with the pain of his sadly punished paws.

Then all together they fell upon the Bear and beat him grievously, but not to his death as the Fox had hoped. For, with the loss of several claws, Bruin managed to pull free and then made off into the Forest, limping heavily, the red blood dripping from his wounds.

And in this sad state he traveled through the night, coming at dawn into the court, where at first, because of

the blood and dust making a mask upon him, he was no
known. Then in a weak and piteous voice he told his tale
and all were astounded at this new proof of the Fox':
wickedness.

But the King thought privately that part of the Bear':
ill luck was of his own making, since he had trusted so easily
in the words of the Fox. And the Lion resolved that the
next messenger he should send would be one of quicker and
slyer wit, for even deeper grew his determination to bring
this villain to justice and crush such evil out of the Fores
kingdom.

Count Lupus was secretly pleased at the Bear's plight
for he greatly hated the Fox and now he believed that the
Bear would join him in this hatred and that together two
such powerful lords could utterly wipe out the fellow. And
so he said when he visited the Bear, where he lay sick and
stricken, attended by his daughter and her ladies.

But listening to this conference was Squire Weasel
and he was filled with fear for Reynard, for he did not se
how the Fox could successfully withstand the King's open
justice and the hidden enmity of the Wolf and the Bear
He went about the court listening to this one and that, hear
ing that many of the smaller folk had much against the Fox
and, were he brought to trial, they would speak out agains
him. Few there were who would support him.

When the Hare proclaimed the court open, Sir Lynx

who was of the Wolf's following, arose and demanded that
the bodyguard of the King be ordered out against Baron
Reynard and that they should not wait for a trial, but should
destroy him utterly and his household with him. But the
Lion shook his head at this, saying that all must be done
seemingly and with order after the rules of the court.

Then he called for one to go out against Reynard and
bring him in. But no one stepped forward. Among the lesser
people there was fear of the Fox, and perhaps there was that
also, secretly, among the great lords. For all remembered in
what plight the Bear had returned to them, and, of them
all, the Bear had been one of the mightiest fighters and one
of the strongest of body.

At last, the Lion lost patience with all of them and
spoke strongly, saying:

'Much has been told here concerning this Fox, who is,
after all, no great lord or holder of some keep well fortified
against all comers. And yet no one of you will now go out
against him to do the will of justice. Can it be that you
fear him?'

Squire Weasel looked from face to face and none that
stood in the ranks of the great lords would make the King
answer, save one. And, when he saw that one step forward,
the Weasel knew real fear, for of them all he seemed the
one best fashioned by Nature to match Baron Reynard's
wit with equal cunning.

Chapter the sixth

WHICH TELLETH HOW DUKE TYBALT
VOLUNTEERED TO REDUCE THE
REBEL AND WHAT HAPPENED THERE-
AFTER

Now this lord never spoke much or raised loud his voice in dispute, but his wisdom was known to all and he was much favored therefore by King Lion, for they were both of the same line and family, he being Duke Tybalt, the Cat. Even now he did not open his sleepy eyes overmuch or seem greatly concerned with the affair, but he said:

'If it be the will of the court to have in this evildoer, then shall I undertake to bring him here, and that speedily.'

Hearing this, the Lion smiled favorably upon Duke Tybalt, bidding him good speed and a swift return. So did the Duke set out to carry the King's message. And, at the selfsame moment, Squire Weasel again slipped away to warn his friend.

Reynard and his lady wife were yet laughing and making merry over the fate of Bruin and the cleverness of the Baron when the Weasel came to them with the dire news of Tybalt's quest. And at this news the Baron at once lost his good humor and became gravely alert.

'For,' as he said to his wife and the Weasel, 'this is another kettle of fish altogether. Duke Tybalt is no stupid Bear to be mishandled and sent yelping home to his master. He is quick-witted and suspicious, and I must indeed lay deep plans if I am to bring about his undoing.'

'But can you?' asked Squire Weasel.

In answer the Baron smiled. 'I can, Cousin Weasel,

I can. For I am not like the other Forest dwellers. There are in me the seeds of greatness and in time I shall rule this world, as all shall learn. Have I not already flouted King Lion and not suffered for it? And have I not conquered the Bear whom all—even the Wolf—secretly fear? You say that the Bear and the Wolf now plot against me—well, let them! I shall yet have the hide of one as a rug for my feet and the pads of the other to make me boots. But first I shall deal with Duke Tybalt in a way never to be forgotten while fox or cat walks the Forest roads. Get you gone now, good Weasel, for none must yet guess that we think alike in this and all other matters. But soon will come the day when all shall know which are my friends and which are my foes, and those who are the latter shall wish bitterly that they were the former.'

Thus again Squire Weasel slipped away secretly while Reynard went to stand by his gate and await the Duke. But Lady Fox took her cubs and hid in a far corner of the manor, for she believed that this time her husband had met his match.

Tybalt saw Reynard awaiting him and thought: That fellow is planning some trickiness, even as he planned the downfall of the Earl Marshal. But this time he shall discover that he has one of a different sort with whom to deal.

And brusquely he bade the Fox make ready and ride back to court with him. Meekly Reynard agreed at once

to go. But he asked that first they both might break their
fast and that he might bid farewell to his lady wife. And
he spoke with such a humble, trembling voice that the Cat
believed him far sunk in fear.

'I know, my lord,' said Reynard, 'that the King and
all the court believed that the Earl Marshal came to evil
through me. But that is not so. I warned him against the
trap which was set before the hives, but in his haste to get
at the honey he did just as I said not to do and so was caught.'

Duke Tybalt blinked his eyes and thought that perhaps
that tale might be true. For all knew that Bruin was so
greedy for honey that he would take any risk to get it. And
in his haste he might well have misunderstood the Fox's
directions. After all, when you saw this fox he did not look
so black a villain as all would have you believe him. And
so was Duke Tybalt partly disarmed of his suspicions, and
he listened more closely when the Fox continued:

'I have but plain rude fare, unsuitable for such a lord
as you. But a short distance down that path is the granary
of a Man. And going into it to feed upon the grain are such
fat rats as you, my lord, have never seen, not even served up
at the King's table. Nor need you fear aught from the anger
of the Man should you venture in to catch one or two, for
you are not stealing what he values for his own use — as
was Bruin when he raided the hives — but instead are you
not doing him a service? And between cats and Men there

is not war as with most of us Forest people. Are not many of your close kindred good friends of Men, dwelling even at their firesides and sharing with them their food?'

The Duke nodded. 'That is the truth which you speak. And these rats are fat, say you?'

'Aye. So fat that their skins are stretched nigh unto bursting. Even as short a time ago as yesterday did I hear the Man lamenting that he had none of your kin to help him be rid of them. Go and try your luck there, my lord, while I prepare to accompany you back to court.'

Tybalt considered the matter but could not see that there was any danger in such an undertaking. It was true that he had no quarrel with Men and that rats were the prey of both. Perhaps the Fox knew that he could not fool such a one as the Cat and wished in this way to buy his favor. Well, if that were his plan it would not profit him.

So the Duke went on down the road in search of the granary and its fat rats.

Chapter the seventh

WHICH TELLETH HOW IT CHANCED
WITH TYBALT AND KING LION'S
WRATH THEREFOR

The granary stood on a little hillock but its door was stoutly barred and locked so that the Duke needs must go around its walls seeking an entrance. And in so doing he came upon a mound of fresh earth from a burrow which led under the foundations of the building. Blithely he entered into this and, although the earthen walls were tight about him, he wriggled through to come up within.

But as he came out upon the hard-packed floor a net dropped about him so that he was well caught in its meshes and the more he struggled to free himself, the more entangled he became. Outside the burrow the Fox stood listening. And when he heard the startled cries and struggles of Tybalt, he ran to the house of the Man who owned the granary and beat lustily upon the door, shouting:

'Hola! Hola! Your granary thief is safely caught. Out, neighbor, and deal with him!'

So the Man and his two sons came running, clubs in their hands, and opened the granary door. Within it was dark and they could not see what manner of animal it was caught in their net, only that some animal was struggling therein. So they beat Tybalt with their clubs until he screamed out for mercy and in his frenzy tore so at the cords of the net that he won free and fled out of the door, his whole body battered and bleeding. Thus again was Reynard disappointed and his enemy escaped the sure death he had planned for him.

It took many long hours for Tybalt to drag himself back to court and when he came all were roused by his story. He himself was bowed in shame as well as pain, because he had been so befooled by Reynard, openly proving himself no wiser than stupid Bruin. So that, getting leave from King Lion, he was fain to withdraw from court and go to his own manor to lie and lick his wounds and nurse his hate against the Fox.

While he rested thus Count Lupus came to him and suggested that he make one with the Wolf and the Bear in their plans against Reynard and he agreed weakly. So he spent his hours in dreaming of the revenge they would have when Reynard was at last brought before the King.

But King Lion was enraged so that his roars might be heard almost the full length of the Forest. And he vowed that he would break the Fox even as a woodman breaks a rotten stick. For never before in all history or legend had the ruler of the Great Forest been so defied and his orders so turned to naught. Thus was he now tinder to be set afire by the suggestions of Count Lupus.

The Weasel saw and heard all and his fears for his friend mounted high. For it was in the King's mind to send out the full might of the court to crush Reynard without pity. Then did the Squire think to try the last hope of all. And, greatly daring, he came alone, and very humbly, to the foot of the throne, there making a low obeisance. When the King acknowledged him and bade him speak, he did so meekly, but with reason and sense.

'My King and lords, well do we all know how ill Baron Reynard has behaved in this and other matters and that it is right that he should be brought to justice. But in all our history no animal has been judged to the death when he was not here to plead for himself and give his side of the story. Therefore, I beg you, do not in your righteous wrath put aside our customs and deal fatally with the Fox until he stands before you——'

'Willingly enough would we wait to deal justice openly,' returned King Lion. 'But Baron Reynard comes not when asked civilly and also does he deal most despitefully with our messengers. Therefore the rogue must face the consequences of such deeds.'

'That is most true. But again, I pray you, my most noble King, let us try once more to bring him forth peacefully. Fear ruled him when you sent first the Earl Marshal, the most powerful of your lords, and then Duke Tybalt, your own good cousin. And when fear rules a heart its owner does wild things to save himself. Therefore this time send some weak, small animal to reason with Baron Reynard. Send me if it be your royal will!'

For a moment the Lion thought, and it seemed to him that Squire Weasel had reasoned well. At least it would do no harm to try his plan. So at last the King agreed, much to the surprise and dismay of Count Lupus, and the Weasel set out.

Chapter the eighth

WHICH TELLETH HOW SQUIRE WEASEL
PLAYED THE HERALD AND GAVE
GOOD ADVICE

For the third time Squire Weasel came unto Fox Manor and spoke with its lord. But this time he was glum of face and spoke warningly.

'The King's wrath is indeed high against you, Baron Reynard. And those you have dealt with are urging him to wait no longer, but to crush you without trial. Therefore I beseech you to put aside all pride and come to court and there make a moan for pardon, for naught else can save you now.'

'What care I for the King's pardon? Have I not routed his two greatest lords, all without risking an inch of my skin? So will I rout the King himself if he comes——'

Squire Weasel shook his head. 'There is a time to be prideful and a time to walk humbly. Put aside your pride now, that it may cloak you on another day. For wits cannot save you if all the Forest turns against you and hunts you down. Our King desires above all else to be thought just. He will pardon any misdoer who repents openly and for-swears his sins. It is your only chance.'

Baron Reynard was not so puffed up with pride that he did not see the good sense in what the Weasel had said. But it hurt him full sore to agree. However, he thought privately, he might walk humbly before the King to save his skin now, and in a later time have another accounting which would profit him far more.

So he put off his fine garments and donned a cloak of

gray sackcloth such as professed sinners wore. His lady wife lamented much, for she was sure that never again would she see his face. But he bade her keep heart, for all was not yet lost, and he had several fine tricks yet to play.

Then he and the Weasel set off for court, both walking in the dust of the road as becomes common folk who make no pretense of rank or pride. And so they came at last into the court. And there was much outcry when Baron Reynard was sighted. Sticks and stones were thrown, as well as foul names cried, until those of the King's guard cleared a path leading to the throne.

Down this paced the Fox, his head bowed upon his paws. And from his eyes dripped tears to wet his coarse robe. And ever and anon he moaned aloud as if with inner pain. Thus he came and threw himself at the King's feet, beating his head and paws on the earth, so did he humble himself.

Behind the King's throne Count Lupus stood with gleaming eyes, for now he saw the end of his long fight and his enemy delivered into his power. But King Lion was startled at the Fox's actions, for he had thought that if Reynard came at all it would be as a hardened villain dragged in against his will, and not as a weeping penitent.

'Mercy, O most just King,' the Fox cried aloud. 'Grant a most miserable sinner mercy, of your bounty. I have done much evil. But also have my enemies magnified what I have done so that I have been sore afraid of coming hither. For who am I to speak against the words of your great lords?'

'Here all have a voice, even the meanest varlet,' returned the Lion sternly. 'And each has the right to speak, be he lord or commoner.'

'True. But if one has powerful enemies who wish to discredit him, may they not send out many to witness against him? — To get up and speak in open court so that his deeds seem much blacker than they were? So has it been done with me——'

'Do you accuse any here of testifying falsely?' demanded the Lion.

'I have not heard what was said, O mighty one! So how can I know whether it was false or true?'

The Lion then turned to the Hare and commanded that the charges which had been made against the Fox be read aloud. And the Hare did so, giving first the story of Count Lupus concerning the villainy practiced upon his poor wife, and then the plea for justice which Sir Chanticleer had raised above his daughter's coffin. And last of all he added the tales told by Bruin and Tybalt upon their separate returns from acting as the King's messenger.

And to all who heard the Hare's reading it seemed a very black record indeed.

Chapter the ninth

WHICH TELLETH HOW BARON REYNARD MADE HIS PEACE WITH A FORKED TONGUE

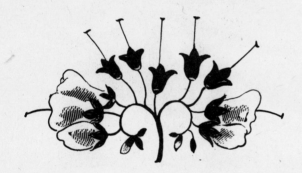

W

hat answer have you to make to these charges, Baron Reynard?' asked King Lion when the Herald was done.

'Many answers, O King, if you will have the patience to hear me out. First — the affair of my Lady Wolf. For long and long, my lord, has Count Lupus been an enemy of mine and wished me ill openly, as I can prove by witnesses, if it so please the court. Now this story of his wife has another side.

'It is true that I went fishing in the river and was well rewarded. While I was yet there my Lady Wolf came hither and sat down to watch me at my working, jeering at my labor, saying that it was only fit employ for varlets of the household and not for gentlefolk. But I am a poor man and I have few varlets to so serve me. And while she sat here the ice did form about her tail and clip her fast. When she discovered what had happened to her, she did cry out most mightily. But I could not free her, not having the strength. So I ran for help. While I was so gone a party of Men came upon her and treated her as they treat any of her kind when they catch them. But none of this was my fault, I most humbly submit.

'As for the death of Sir Chanticleer's daughter — for that I am most heartily sorry. It is true that I did frequent his family and eat at his board. All here know how esteemed is this fine old knight and how pleasant it is to be in his company. And I did chance upon little Pippet in the garden.

She took fright at my coming upon her so suddenly, for she was always a timorous maid. But when I would soothe her gently she became quite mad with fear, throwing herself first this way and then that, so I did seize firmly upon her lest she do herself a grave injury, and, alas, then her terror mounted until it broke her heart and she died. When I tried to explain this to those of her household they drove me forth at the fear of my life and would not listen to aught I had to say. And that I swear is the true story of Pippet's death — upon my heart's blood I swear it!

'As for the sad mishaps of the Earl Marshal and Duke Tybalt, they are to blame for their fates themselves. The Earl Marshal went to steal honey and was caught in a trap which I myself had warned him against. Nor can his greed or clumsiness be called sins of mine.

'Duke Tybalt would have been welcomed by the owner of the granary had he gone to the door and asked properly for a chance to hunt down the rats. Instead he crept in slyly and so was caught in a net laid against thieves. For his bad judgment I surely cannot be held accountable. So it is in my mind that I am more unfortunate than truly wicked, many as my sins may be.'

All this he said in a low, respectful voice, the tears dropping from his eyes and sobs rising to break his words. And many of those who heard were impressed by his distress. Also his stories, being founded upon a germ of real truth, did not sound so ill. It was hard to believe him such a black rogue as he had been painted.

Even King Lion began to wonder whether he had not been deceived by anger. And so he determined not to be too hasty in judging the Fox. But Count Lupus was wrathful when he saw the effect of Baron Reynard's fine speech and he was afraid that the Fox would escape proper punishment after all.

For a long time the King sat in silence and when he spoke all listened to him eagerly.

'It seems to me that true repentance should be encouraged and the sinner not made more miserable by unduly harsh punishment. Also it is true that there is an element of chance in this case. Perhaps Baron Reynard has been the victim of fate somewhat, even as he has said. Therefore he shall go in humiliation and suffering but his life shall remain in his body.

'This, then, is my sentence. That he shall leave the Forest and go as a pilgrim to a far shrine of the Menfolk. And he shall do this as go the meanest varlets, in sackcloth and begging his food. And for a year and a day the Forest shall not know him, nor shall he look upon the face of any who dwell here. And that this order may be strictly obeyed, my Chief Herald Hare and Bishop Ram shall go with him to the edge of the Forest and see him forth from our borders. I have spoken!'

But great was the anger of Count Lupus at that, and great was the fear of the smaller animals upon whose kind Baron Reynard had preyed. For once none were pleased with King Lion's justice.

Chapter the tenth

WHICH TELLETH HOW THE FOX
BEGAN HIS PILGRIMAGE AND OF
THE SAD FATE OF THE HARE

When Reynard heard the King's sentence he wept aloud and cried out between choking sobs that it was only just and he would obey. But King Lion ordered the Hare, his Chief Herald, and Bishop Ram to accompany the Fox to the edge of the Forest and there see him out into the world. And Reynard, in the sackcloth of a penitent sinner, set off meekly with this chosen escort.

But once outside the court he turned to them and said, in a meek and fearful voice:

'My lords, I pray you, out of the goodness of your pitiful hearts, let me pass by Fox Manor on my way hence so that I may speak with my lady wife and let her know how it fares with me. Otherwise she will mourn me as one dead and naught will comfort her. And allow me once more to see my children, flesh of my flesh and bone of my bone, so that I may carry such a memory of them deep within me.'

The Hare bethought himself of his own young family and how he would like to be dealt with in such a case, and he speedily agreed, while Bishop Ram, who was good but of simple wit, could see no harm in granting the Fox this boon.

Accordingly they turned aside from the King's highway and came to Fox Manor. There Baron Reynard stopped short by the gate and addressed Bishop Ram:

'If your worship would be so kind as to linger here in the shade of my garden trees I shall send forth a varlet with a cooling drink for your throat. But let the noble Hare come with me that he may explain to my wife this dread order of the King's.'

The Bishop, who was no longer young, and who was indeed tired and thirsty, and who most of all disliked seeing the tears of Lady Fox, allowed himself to be persuaded. So he sat on a bench under the trees while Reynard and the Hare went within.

Reynard's wife came running to embrace him, crying:

'My lord, how has it chanced with you? How has the King dealt with you?'

Then did the Fox tell her of the punishment the King had laid upon him. And she began to wail and cry out upon their fate, saying:

'If you are gone from us, how shall we then live? Already is the larder bare and there is naught to fill the empty stomachs of our sons. Will you leave us thus to starve? Ah woeful, woeful day this is!'

'Nay, good wife, moan not,' the Fox answered her, 'for I have brought with me meat such as we have not had served up in many a long day.'

'Meat, say you? Where?'

'Here!' cried the Baron, and leaped upon the Hare beating him to earth and snapping his neck.

Then the wicked two dragged the body into their larder and stowed it away therein. But Reynard cut free the Hare's head and put it in a leathern bag.

'Do not fear,' he said when this was done. 'I shall go with the Bishop to the edge of the Forest. But after he has seen me on my way he will go to report to the King. Then shall I too slip back into the Forest and will come here. All will think me gone and we can live quietly here without notice until I can take vengeance on those who have turned the King against me.'

So saying he took the bag with the Hare's head in it and went out to the Bishop. He told the Ram that his wife had swooned in her sorrow and that the Hare had promised to remain with her and grant her such comfort as he could.

Along the way to the edge of the wood many and deep were the Fox's sighs so that the kind-hearted Ram was deeply sorry for him and tried to lighten his spirits by saying that the year of the King's displeasure would not last forever, and that he could then return to those he loved.

And when they came to the parting of their roads, the Fox handed to the Ram the leathern bag which contained the Hare's head. And with the bag he laid upon the Bishop a task, saying:

'To show King Lion how much I am in his debt, give this unto him, not opening it until you stand before his throne so that all may see what I think of the King's high justice.'

And the Ram agreed to do even as the Fox had asked.

Chapter the eleventh

WHICH TELLETH HOW BISHOP RAM
DELIVERED THE BAG TO THE
KING AND A GALLOWS IS BUILT

The Ram watched the Fox trudge out of sight, then he retraced his way back to court. There all was merriment and feasting, for the animals believed that the villain Fox was safely out of the Forest for a year. Only Count Lupus, Earl Marshal Bruin, and Duke Tybalt kept their own counsel and thought dark thoughts, because they believed that the Forest had not yet lost that slippery-tongued rascal. Nor did they think that the Baron's repentance was a true one.

When the Bishop came unto the King he offered the bag, saying that it contained a gift which Baron Reynard had sent to show his respect for the justice of the Lion. And, at the King's nod, the Ram loosed the knots and shook out the contents.

So did the bloody head of the Hare, he who had been the Chief Herald of the court, roll to his master's feet.

At the horror of that sight all stood frozen until the Lion arose with a great roar of wrath and demanded of the silly, shaking Ram the story of how this crime had been done.

In a thin and stammering voice Bishop Ram told how Reynard had begged him to stay in the garden and refresh himself while the King's Herald went within the manor to pacify Lady Fox. And how, when Reynard had come out alone, he said that the Hare, because of his kindness, had stayed behind to comfort his wife. He ended by repeating, as well as he could remember, the words with which the Fox had left him the bag.

'Thou peaked fool!' shouted the Lion. 'Wits you have none! Does this black villain Fox possess all the wits of the kingdom within his head that he can so easily befool all my greatest lords?'

Count Lupus grinned sourly and bethought himself that the Fox had befooled the Lion also with his talk. But he knew that the King would never admit that. However, the Wolf rejoiced at the Lion's rage, for he believed that this time surely the Fox would not escape death.

And true did that seem, for within the hour the King ordered that a gallows be built on the nearest hillock and he sent those of his own guard to find and bring back Baron Reynard.

Meanwhile the Fox had re-entered the Forest and was going to his manor by hidden ways so that he might not be seen. But there was a Crow, old and crippled, who had not gone to court because of his age and infirmities. Age and a crippled leg had not taken his curiosity from him, however, and he was interested in all that he could see from his tree house.

So had he watched carefully the Bishop and the Baron pass on their way to the edge of the Forest. And then he had witnessed the Ram's open return, and later spied upon the Fox's secret one. So interested did he become in all this that he left his doorsill, which he had not done for many a day before, and fluttered along from branch to branch, keeping the Fox in sight until he entered the gate of Fox Manor.

The Crow then perched near-by in a tree to consider the inner meaning of what he had seen, and so was he still sitting when the guardsmen of the King came by. It was their intention to try to learn from Lady Fox something of her husband's plans. But when they beat upon the door she called out shrilly that she would not unbar the gate nor allow them to enter, being now a lone woman without her lord to defend her.

While she so held them, Baron Reynard slipped out through a side postern and went into the Forest. Only the Crow marked his going and the path he took. And having no reason to love Baron Reynard, the old bird called softly to the leader of the guard, telling him what he had seen.

Thus, leaving two of his following to do sentry duty before the gate of Fox Manor, the Captain sent his men into the Forest and before long they surrounded and captured the Fox. This time they loaded him with chains as they were wont to do with evildoers of the common sort.

With the Fox so bound in their midst they set out for court. And long before they reached the quarters of King Lion they could hear the loud hammer-blows of those who were building a gallows for Baron Reynard.

Chapter the twelfth

WHICH TELLETH HOW DAME MONKEY
CAME TO REYNARD IN PRISON AND
WHAT CHANCED THEREFOR

As hopeless as Baron Reynard's lot now seemed, he did not lack for secret friends and among these was Dame Monkey, a lady who served as nurse for the King's youngest cub. Being quick of wit and able at flattery she was held in high esteem by Queen Lioness and, after Baron Reynard had been placed in the best guarded of the prison cells, she went to her mistress to plead thus:

'My liege lady, I pray you of your great kindness, allow me to pass the prison guards and console this wretched Fox. In older and happier days his wife was a friend of my bosom and ofttimes have I feasted at Fox Manor. This being so, it is only right that I should now do what I can for an old friend come to this black fate.'

Queen Lioness believed Dame Monkey and smiled upon her, saying to her other ladies:

'It is right that old friends should not be readily deserted when they fall into misfortune. Although this Fox is a notorious rogue and richly deserves his fate, however, I freely grant you, Dame Monkey, permission to console him in his cell.'

Thus Dame Monkey won her way into the prison and was brought into Baron Reynard's cell where she found him looking forth from a high window upon the gallows which had been so newly built.

'How now, Reynard!' she began. 'Wracked with sorrow I am in truth to discover you in this cruel trap. If there be aught that I can do to make your last hours the easier you have but to speak forth and it shall be done.'

But the Fox shook his head. 'My course seems fully run,' he said quietly enough. 'And the King's justice will be served. So let us say no more concerning the matter. Instead, I pray you, Sister Monkey, tell me of court matters that I may lighten my mind and forget what comes tomorrow.'

So did she give him all the tittle-tattle of the court and all the gossip she had gathered. For Dame Monkey had made it her business to learn all she could of the private affairs of her fellow courtiers. And at last she told the Fox a story which interested him very much.

It seemed that King Lion, while walking the Forest, had trodden flat a city of the Ant people and now they were aroused to wrath because he had not made any excuse for such discourtesy. Baron Reynard, hearing of this, stopped Dame Monkey in mid-word and cried eagerly:

'Sister Monkey, if you truly wish my better fortune and my escape from this bitter fate, do you bring hither the strongest fighter among the Ants. Tell them that I can show them a way to be avenged on King Lion. And I shall also save myself into the bargain.'

Dame Monkey thereupon hurried straightway to the nearest Ant city and asked for their strongest fighter, telling them that she could show them a way to be avenged on King Lion. And the Ants, after conferring together, brought forth one of their number who was larger in size and possessed very strong and powerful jaws.

Having stowed the Ant carefully in her belt pouch, Dame Monkey came again to the prison on the pretext of bringing wine and cakes to lighten somewhat Reynard's last hours, and was shown in to him. There she produced the Ant and the Fox was overjoyed.

'This then shall you do to avenge your city,' he told the Ant. 'Dame Monkey will carry you secretly into King Lion's bedchamber and place you on his pillow. Bide there hidden until he retires and then do you come forth and crawl into the inner part of his ear. Once within seize upon the tender flesh and do not let go. The pain of your attack will be fitting punishment for this stern lord.'

The Ant, having agreed readily to this plan, was put back into the pouch by Dame Monkey. But the Fox had yet more instructions for her.

'When the King is sick with pain and his surgeon can give him no relief, then do you use well your wit, Sister Monkey. Make known that my grandfather once suffered from just such an ailment and that he found a cure, the secret of which is now mine alone.'

Dame Monkey's eyes sparkled and she agreed with vigor before going away to put their plan to work.

Chapter the thirteenth

WHICH TELLETH HOW KING LION
WAS STRICKEN IN THE NIGHT AND
DAME MONKEY GAVE ADVICE

It was late before King Lion sought his bed and he was full weary when he stretched himself out thereon. But the Ant had not slept and as soon as the King's heavy head was on the pillow, the fighter crept, as he had been instructed, into the tender inner part of the Lion's ear. And there with his jaws he fastened upon the flesh so that the Lion sat up on his bed with a loud roar of honest pain.

Rudely awakened by his cries, the Lioness implored him to tell her what ailed him, and courtiers and guards burst in at the door to stand amazed about the bed. Now the Lion shook his head from side to side and dug at his tormented ear with his paw. But the Ant was too far in to be so dislodged. Tears of torment rolled from the King's eyes and he begged help of them all.

The Goat, who was court surgeon, had been summoned with all haste and now came bustling in, dragging his robe over his shoulders, so quickly had he come. But he could do nothing that eased his master. While he was working so fruitlessly, Dame Monkey approached the Lioness and ventured to twitch the long sleeve of her night robe.

'My dearest lady,' she said in a low voice so that only the Queen might hear, 'once before have I seen such an illness——'

'Where and when?' demanded the Queen.

'It was at Fox Manor many years ago when I was but a young child. Old Baron Reynard, the grandfather of him

who now waits the King's justice, was so stricken in th
night and long did he suffer torture. But at last he foun
a remedy——'

'What was it?' cried the Lioness.

'That I do not know, my lady, for he would never tel
But doubtless he left some word concerning it to member
of his own family — perchance to this very rogue now withi
prison.'

Then did the Queen pour out to the King the whol
tale told her by Dame Monkey, urging him mightily to sen
for Baron Reynard and discover if indeed the Fox had th
cure for such a grievous ailment. And the Lion, driven hal
mad by pain, was willing to do anything or send for anyon
who might ease him. Accordingly he ordered that Reynar
be instantly brought to him.

When the Fox was roused from sleep by the jailer an
ordered to accompany the King's guard to the palace h
knew that his plan was working and on the way he schemec
as to how he could best rid himself of all his more powerfu
enemies and gain the King's favor, all in a single night. Bu
although his heart sang his face was downcast and he walkec
with the dragging steps of one who has not long to live.

Still in the midst of the guard he was brought into th
bedchamber of the King and the roars of the tortured Lior
were sweet music to him. When he came into sight th
Lioness addressed him at once.

'I have been told that one of your family once suffered
from this disorder and cured himself. Is that true?'

'It is, even as you have said, great lady. My grand
father was taken with such a pain in the middle of the night,
as was your lord. And he recovered himself of it. So that
none of his household might be so stricken again, he wrote
down the ingredients of the medicine he used, and I found
it not long ago among his old papers. Now I say to you, my
lady, although I lie under your lord's great displeasure, I
shall use this remedy in his behalf, if he will have it so.'

'Use it at once,' ground out the King between locked
teeth, for the pain seemed almost more than he could bear.

'Very well.' The Fox became brisk and elbowed aside
the helpless surgeon Goat who had been nearest the Lion.
But I shall need many things——'

'Give him whatever he wants!' ordered the Lion.

'I shall need,' continued Baron Reynard, his eyes glint
ing evilly, 'the freshly flayed skin of a bear, the four feet of
a wolf, and the eyes of a cat.'

And as he said these words a silence fell upon all the
assembly, but the Lion had only half heard.

'Give him whatever he wants,' he moaned to his guards.

Chapter the fourteenth

WHICH TELLETH HOW SQUIRE HOUND CAME TO SUSPECT REYNARD AND ACTED THEREUPON

ow among those courtiers who had come into the King's chamber when he had cried out in his great pain was Squire Hound, a follower of Count Lupus and distantly of his kin. He was keen of both wit and ear and he had no love for Baron Reynard. So when the Fox made his monstrous demand for the four feet of a wolf, Squire Hound suspected that there was no truth in Baron Reynard's claim to knowledge of a secret medicine. He believed that the Fox was using it as a chance to rid himself of his greatest enemies.

Also he did not trust Dame Monkey, having seen her in private converse with Queen Lioness and knowing of her two visits to Reynard in prison. Realizing that whatever he could do to save his friend and kinsman, Count Lupus, must be done quickly, straightway he crossed the chamber and sought out one of the younger maids of honor, Lady Red Deer, saying to her privately:

'While we are waiting for the Fox's medicine to be made, there is one other remedy which may be tried to relieve our lord. Do you speak with your mistress — softly, lest Dame Monkey hear — and suggest that hot oil be poured into the ear. I have known this to help in such cases.'

Lady Red Deer was no friend of Dame Monkey, who, by her spiteful gossip, had harmed many of the court ladies. And although she did not know why Squire Hound wished this of her, she knew him to be an honest and

brave young animal and felt sure that he meant the Kin
no hurt.

So she went speedily to the side of her mistress an
said:

'My lady, the royal prince, your youngest cub, is cry
ing loudly for his nurse and none but Dame Monkey ca
console him ——'

So, much against her will, Dame Monkey needs mus
hurry away to the royal nursery, leaving Lady Red Dee
with the queen. And the maid of honor made good use c
her opportunity, saying at once:

'Since our lord's pain and suffering are so great tha
all who see him needs must share it, I venture to suggest
remedy which may bring him temporary relief. Let oil b
warmed and then poured into his ear.'

The Lioness was willing to try anything which migh
aid her mate, so it was straightway done and she dipped th
hot oil into his ear with her own hand. Now when the o
ran into the inner ear the Ant was trapped and, sore frigh
ened, loosened its grip, so that when the Lion shook his hea
the insect was flung out with the oil.

And at once the Lion was freed from pain. But Squir
Hound, who had quietly pushed forward to stand close b
the bed, saw the Ant, caught in the sticky oil, fall upon th
King's pillow.

'There' — he raised his voice so that all talking stoppe

...d everyone looked toward the spot where he pointed — 'is
...e miscreant who has so sorely used our lord. See that Ant
...apped in the oil which dripped from the King's ear——'

Baron Reynard knew then that his plans had gone
...vry and, as the others crowded around the bed to look at
...quire Hound's discovery, he edged away toward the window
...d leaped out. None noted his going.

'This was some evil plan of that villain Fox,' cried
...quire Hound. 'I pray you, my lord, take back your cruel
...der that the good Bear must lose his skin, that my kinsman
...ust shed his feet and the Cat his eyes to cure you.'

When the Lion understood what he had unknowingly
...dered in his pain, he sent guards running to save his faith-
...l followers and it was then that those within the room dis-
...vered that Baron Reynard had also left without taking
...rmal leave of the court.

Squire Hound fell upon his knees at the side of the
...d and said earnestly:

'I ask it humbly of your highness, my lord, that you
...ant me leave to hunt down this twice- and thrice-cursed
...llain and bring him to justice. The Great Forest will
...ever be happy or peaceful again while he and those of his
...ood remain within its borders.'

The Lion stripped his ring of state from his claw and
...anded it to Squire Hound.

'Let it be so,' he ordered. 'Wearing this you shall deal

the King's justice and none shall refuse you aid. Rid us of this wretch as quickly as you can.'

Thus, with the King's guardsmen at his tail, Squire Hound rode forth to hunt down Baron Reynard and all those of his blood.

Chapter the fifteenth

WHICH TELLETH HOW FOX MANOR
WAS DESERTED AND SQUIRE HOUND
SPOKE · WITH · THE · CROW

aron Reynard had traveled fast, for the fear of swift death spurred him, and when he reached the door of his own manor he was sore spent. But there he stayed only long enough to summon his wife and their cubs, and then his little party fled by the secret postern gate into a part of the Great Forest which was wild and lonely and had no roads. There the Fox sought out a certain cave which had a very narrow opening, so narrow that he and his wife could just squeeze through.

But this cave had also another deeply hidden entrance and so Reynard felt secure, for if Squire Hound and his friends should find the first entrance, the Fox family could escape by the rear. But he did not know that the Crow had marked his going and had then flown back to the tree by Fox Manor gate.

As Squire Hound and his guards came riding up, the Crow called out to the leader:

'Good Squire, he whom you seek has gone away with his wife and cubs.'

'Did you chance to mark the direction of their going?' cried the Hound.

'Aye, that I did. They lie secure within a cave and you cannot have them forth, for if you force the front entrance then will they escape by the back. It is the nature of the Fox family never to seek a refuge which has not two exits.'

Squire Hound knew that the Crow spoke true. But he

was determined to outwit the Fox, so now he dismounted and
ordered his guards to do likewise. And with the help of one
of the varlets he loosed off his mail and half armor so that he
could move quickly and without sound. Even his sword he
put aside, keeping only the long dagger at his belt.

Then he said to the Crow:

'Out of your kindness, Brother Crow, lead me secretly
to this den where Reynard has taken cover that I may spy
out the land.'

This the Crow did and the Hound was able to see that
Reynard had indeed gone to earth in a place where it would
be hard to have him forth. But he also noted that near the
cave was a stream and as he watched the flowing water, a plan
began to take shape in his mind.

'Good Brother Crow, are there others among the feath
ered ones who are like unto you — too old, or too young, to
attend at court?'

The Crow nodded. 'Aye. Perhaps the number of the
claws on my old feet.'

'Can you summon them hither and have them search
hereabouts for the Fox's back door?'

The Crow laughed. 'Right well will they come to
such a task. Baron Reynard wins no love from the feath
ered ones. And my wishes count for much.' So off he flew
to post his watchers.

But Squire Hound went back to his guards. There he

ade them doff their armor and, with only their swords,
ollow him through the Forest. Three of them he set to
eaving, with tough vines, a large net, and the rest he set to
gging in the soft earth a trench leading from the stream to
e mouth of the cave where the Fox and his family lay
idden.

Now the Fox was watching them from within the cave
d he was astounded and wrathful that they had discovered
is hiding-place so quickly, for he knew nothing about the
row. But he said to his wife:

'Do not fear, my sweet. Let them sweat and dig.
Vhen they have accomplished their purpose, tiring them-
lves greatly meantime, then shall we be out and off by the
ack way and leave them with their paws as empty as their
eads. Go you now and put our cubs at the exit so that we
n get them forth speedily.'

She did as he bade her. Taking their cubs into the far
aches of the cave, and leaving them at the opening with
rict warning not to look forth, she hurried back to the
de of her lord.

But the cubs were small and did not understand why
ey had been brought from their comfortable home into
is dark hole in the ground, and they did not like the rough
ve and the darkness. So when they saw the sunlight out-
de they edged toward it and the smaller one thrust out his
ead to sniff the fresh, warm air.

He was at once spied by a young Robin who had bee
posted thereabouts to watch for just such a happening. An
when the larger cub, who was more cautious, pulled th
smaller back, the Robin flew off and told the Crow what l
had seen. In this manner did Squire Hound learn the loc
tion of the Fox's secret entrance. Thus he was able to s
his trap accordingly.

Chapter the sixteenth

WHICH TELLETH HOW BARON REYNARD WAS OUTWITTED AND SQUIRE HOUND GAINED MUCH FAME THEREAFTER

Under the eye of Baron Reynard the guards worked hard at their digging and Squire Hound himself did not disdain to help scoop up the earth. The Fox took much pleasure in watching this hard labor which he was sure would come to naught, so that he was not willing to leave, although his timorous wife urged him to it repeatedly.

At long length the ditch was dug and Squire Hound gave the signal to allow the water to flow into it and the liquid slopped over the edge and came into the cave, rising about the feet of Baron Reynard and his wife.

'Look to these fools,' he bade his lady. 'See how they think to force us out to face them. We can now be out the back way and over the hills before they even suspect us to be gone.'

So the Baron and his wife retreated into the far part of the cave and there found their cubs and pushed them on ahead. But the water rose faster than Baron Reynard had thought possible, so that he and his wife each caught up one of the children and plunged out of the back opening in some haste, without looking well as to what lay before them.

And thus they blundered headlong into the net of vines which Squire Hound had set to catch them after the Crow had borne him the news of the secret exit. And, terrified, they struggled against the vines, only to entangle themselves the more, even as had Duke Tybalt in the granary.

Then out of the bushes came Squire Hound and his

guards. Seeing his mortal enemy so close Reynard tore fre
in one last wild leap. But, when he saw that his wife an
children could not follow, he returned to aid them and so wa
set upon by Squire Hound.

Long did they battle and then did Baron Reynard a
last meet his match. For here was not a war of wits, but onl
strength against strength. And Squire Hound was young
while Reynard was older and plump and short of breat
with much rich living. Also he had not had to use fan
against one of equal strength for years past, preferring t
attack only those weaker than himself.

So Squire Hound overbore him and he was trusse
up by those who came to serve the King's justice upon hir

Leading the Fox family, all in bonds, the Squire an
his guardsmen returned to court. And all marveled at h
coming and at his cunning when he had told his tale.

Then did King Lion say unto the Fox: 'Villain, nov
do you earn the reward for your deeds. The Hangman waits

But although he deemed all lost now, and he knev
that he stood in the doorway of shameful death, Baron Rey
nard still cried aloud for a chance to be heard, his eyes gleam
ing red with hate and bitterness.

'Kill me, if that be your will, great King,' he spat ou
'and take pleasure in the slaying. But forget not that th
long trial of our wits shall linger in the memories of all beast
and in years to come there shall be those who will rise in cour

say that there are two sides to every question and that in
me of this business the shadow of right lay upon my side.

'Let not those of your great lords plume themselves
my downfall. Although they wished my undoing, it was
t one of them who brought me here in this guise. I am
lled down by this blundering Hound who is but a humble
uire in the train of him whose hate is blackest against me.
herefore I go to death willingly enough, for my shame is
at that my wits could not save me against so low a clown.'

And tears of rage and humiliation wet the thick fur
his snout. Then King Lion guessed that for the Fox
ere was a worse fate than death itself, and that was to live
d remember the shame of his taking by Squire Hound. So
decreed thus:

'Since justice must be served, we shall put an end to
u and those of your house within the Great Forest, but it
all be done in this wise. Get you gone away from here,
king all of your blood with you. Never may you again
turn, nor shall you take on your backs or in your belts
ght of the treasure in your coffers. But from this time
rth you shall earn your bread like the thief and ill-liver
at you are — in another place. Get beyond our borders
d make what peace you can with the race of Man.

'And this also do I now say, that from this hour those
your race be subject to Squire Hound. And Squire Hound
d those of his blood who come after him shall be free to

hunt down a Fox wherever and whenever they may sight
see one, thus providing our kingdom with a guard agair
such villains. So get you away——'

Baron Reynard, anger and shame twisting his mas
followed by his lady wife and their cubs, went forth fro
the court and no more were they or their kind seen the
But Squire Hound was much thought of, being a prin
favorite with his great kinsman Count Lupus, and comir
to high honor with the King.

To this day, although King Lion and his reign be lor
forgot, those of hound blood still hunt the fox and his kin
nor will they cast aside that privilege while they run tl
fields of the earth.

As for the Forest folk, they prospered and lived happi
for long, long years, and never again did a rebel dare to que
tion custom and order — not until Man himself came
dispute King Lion's power. But that is another tale a
together.

JUN   1957